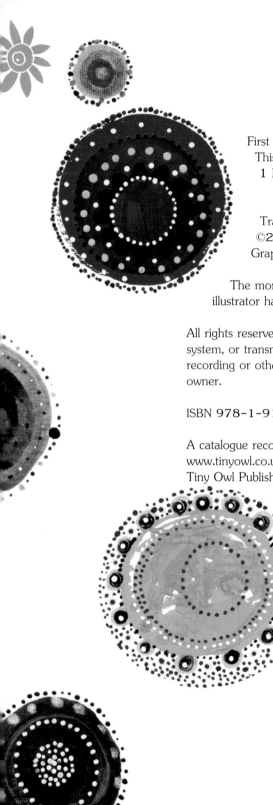
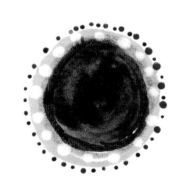

First published in Persian ©2010 Nazar Publisher, Tehran, Iran
This edition published in 2017 by Tiny Owl Publishing Ltd
1 Repton House, Charlwood Street, SW1V 2LD, London, UK

Translated by Azita Rassi
©2015 Tiny Owl Publishing Ltd
Graphic designer: Elahe Javanmard

The moral rights of Ahmadreza Ahmadi as the author and Ehsan Abdollahi as the illustrator have been asserted

ISBN 978-1-910328-22-4

A catalogue record of this book is available from the British Library
www.tinyowl.co.uk
Tiny Owl Publishing Ltd, Registered in England and Wales No. 08297587

tiny owl publishing

When I Coloured in the World

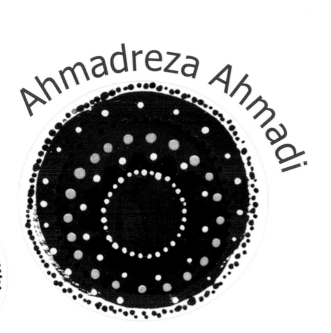

Ahmadreza Ahmadi

Illustrated by Ehsan Abdollahi

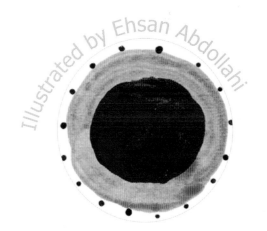

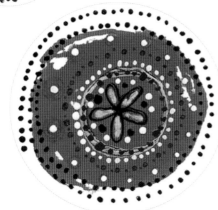

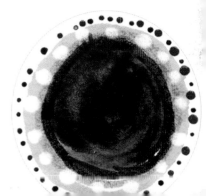

My mum gave me a box of crayons for colouring, and an eraser to rub things out with. So guess what I did?

Desert

I rubbed out the word 'desert'.

I wrote the word 'roses'.

Roses

Red

With my red crayon I made roses grow all over the world!

I gave the world red.

Darkness

I rubbed out the word 'darkness'.
I wrote the word 'light' with my yellow crayon.
Light
Yellow

With my yellow crayon I made lights come
  on all over the world!
I gave the world yellow.

Boredom

I rubbed out that word 'boredom'.

I got my blue crayon and I wrote 'playing'.

Playing

Sky blue

All over the world people played.

I gave the world sky blue.

Drought

I rubbed out that word 'drought'.
I wrote 'rain' with my silver crayon.
Rain
Silver
I made it rain all over the world, and
   everyone had to put up umbrellas!
I gave the world silver.

Hunger

I rubbed out that word 'hunger'.
I wrote 'wheat' with my green crayon.
Green
Wheat
I made wheat grow in fields all over
  the world.
I gave the world green.

War

I rubbed out that word 'war'.
I got my sky blue crayon and I wrote 'peace' with it.
Light blue
Peace
All over the world news came from
   radios saying that all the wars had stopped.
After that news, the radios played such lovely
   music that flowers bloomed in empty vases.
I gave light blue to the world.

Winter

I rubbed out the word 'winter'.
I used my orange crayon to write 'spring'.
Orange
Spring
All over the world, snow melted.
Primroses and violets and orange blossom
  flowered
So that children could sleep with a lovely flowery scent all around them.
I gave the world orange.

Noise

I rubbed out the word 'noise'.
I wrote 'song' with my dark blue crayon.
Dark blue
Song
All over the world my song made children so happy
   that they danced.
I gave the world dark blue.

Crying

I rubbed out the word 'crying'.
Instead I wrote 'laughter' with my purple pencil.
Purple
Laughter
Now, all over the world, mothers danced and
  laughed with their children.
I gave the world purple.

Storm

I rubbed out that word 'storm'.

In its place I wrote 'breeze' with my violet pencil.

Violet

Breeze

Around the world people
  opened their doors

They went outside to chat to each other in the sunny breeze.

I gave the world violet.

Illness

I rubbed out the word 'illness'.

I got my pink crayon, and I wrote 'health' instead.

Pink

Health

All over the world people who had been ill were

  suddenly well!

They ran with their friends and were happy.

I gave pink to the world.

Old age

I rubbed out the words 'old' and 'age'.
Instead I used my orange pencil to write 'people'.
Orange
People

And all over the world, nobody minded
  at all whether somebody else was old or young.
They were just interested in each other.

Flood

I rubbed out the word ' *flood* '.

Instead I wrote ' *drizzle* ' with my silver crayon, just
  as I had used it to write 'rain'.

Silver

Drizzle

Around the world, harvests were saved.

Despair

I rubbed out 'despair'.

I wrote 'hope' with my yellow crayon.

Yellow

Hope

All over the world children smiled.

They ran into the fields and up the hills

Looking at the beautiful new life growing all around.

I gave the world hope.

About the book

A beautifully simple story about how creative imagination — through the
use of colour and imagery — can change the world from bad to good.
This book won the Iranian Flying Turtle Medal.

About the author

Ahmadreza Ahmadi is one of the greatest Iranian contemporary poets,
and his storytelling style reflects that. He has written numerous children's
stories, some of which have won major literary awards in Iran.
In 2010 Ahmadreza Ahmadi was among the five short-listed nominees
for the Hans Christian Andersen Award.